To dung Yo

Cath Howe.

The Curse of the Highwayman

Written by Cath Howe

Illustrated by Keino

Published by Pearson Education Limited, Edinburgh Gate, Harlow, Essex, CM20 2JE
Registered company number: 872828

www.pearsonschools.co.uk

Text © Cath Howe 2012

Designed by Bigtop
Original illustrations © Pearson Education Limited 2012
Illustrated by Keino

The right of Cath Howe to be identified as author of this work has been asserted by her in
accordance with the Copyright, Designs and Patents Act 1988.

First published 2012

16 15 14 13 12
10 9 8 7 6 5 4 3 2 1

British Library Cataloguing in Publication Data
A catalogue record for this book is available from the British Library

ISBN 978 0 435 07570 5

Copyright notice

Printed and bound in the UK

Acknowledgements
We would like to thank the children and teachers of Bangor Central Integrated Primary School,
NI; Bishop Henderson C of E Primary School, Somerset; Brookside Community Primary
School, Somerset; Cheddington Combined School, Buckinghamshire; Cofton Primary School,
Birmingham; Dair House Independent School, Buckinghamshire; Deal Parochial School, Kent;
Holy Trinity Catholic Primary School, Chipping Norton; Lawthorn Primary School, North
Ayrshire; Newbold Riverside Primary School, Rugby and Windmill Primary School, Oxford for
their invaluable help in the development and trialling of the Bug Club resources.

Every effort has been made to contact copyright holders of material reproduced in this book.
Any omissions will be rectified in subsequent printings if notice is given to the publisher.

Contents

Chapter 1

"Wow!" we both murmured. We stood there on the pavement, staring.

"Go on, help yourselves. It's all got to go!" the builder said, lounging on the wall. "They're pulling the whole place down in a week or two."

"This place'll be brilliant for props for the play, Zac!" I said, looking at the blackened building. "Better than that car boot sale. We don't have to pay for this stuff!"

All the windows of the wonky-shaped pub were smashed. We picked our way down the path towards the doorway, crunching on the remains of a bonfire, sniffing the charcoal smell.

"Hey, the builder's gone," said Zac, looking back over his shoulder. "He won't know what we're taking."

"He doesn't care; it's all being thrown away," I said, glancing at the boxes and crates outside the door. "Let's go in. I bet the good stuff's inside."

A shadow of doubt flickered across Zac's face, but then he grinned.

"Go on, then."

"Hello!" I called, pushing the door.

It made a low scraping noise and moved about three centimetres.

My heart began thumping like mad. I don't know why; I'm not scared of the dark or anything like that.

Zac stifled a giggle. "I dare you to run in."

I swung round. "What about you?"

Zac shook his head. "I'll wait for you out here."

"You wuss! It's only an old pub." I gave the door a shove and it swung open. I staggered down several steps into darkness.

Cobwebs tangled my mouth and hair. As I brushed them away, a smell hit me; spicy, like Dad's mulled wine at Christmas, but also stale and musty.

I peered around, my eyes getting used to the semi-dark. Wooden beams with slits of daylight loomed over my head. Against

the walls leaned dust-coated benches and
broken stools. But it still looked like a
proper pub behind the bar, with bottles
clipped to the wall and big pulling handles
for beer.

I breathed out slowly. It was just a falling-down pub. But why did the air feel ice cold?

"Woo, wooooo," went a low voice by the door.

I jumped. "Don't be an idiot, Zac. It's OK. There's no one here," I whispered. Why was I whispering?

Zac's grinning face appeared round the door and he crept in. "Wow! This place looks millions of years old!" Zac bent down to investigate one of the piles of crates and boxes.

Yep. Jugs and tankards and things,"
he said. "Brilliant! I'll fill a carrier bag."

While Zac gathered props for our play,
I looked around. I usually like exploring
old buildings. Why did this one make me
shudder? I rubbed my arms. My gaze
landed on a strangely-shaped wooden
box on the floor. It was like a tiny coffin,
wider at one end than the other. It was
such an unusual shape that I suddenly
wanted it for myself. I could imagine it
in my bedroom, on my desk. It would be
perfect for keeping special things in.

9

"What's in there?" asked Zac, pointing at the box. He was staring at it, too.

"No idea."

"Just bring it, Shona. That horrible smell makes me want to throw up. Let's get out of here. I've got plenty of stuff now."

I scooped up the box and we legged it back out into the daylight.

We turned into a couple of mad things, dashing back along the path, laughing.

"Come on Zac!" I shouted and clambered up a stack of old wooden benches, with Zac wobbling behind me.

"Hey, look at that!" Zac was pointing at something high up; a battered wooden pub sign. "It says 'The Noose and Gibbet'."

Below the words was a faded picture. The paint was peeling off, but there was enough to make out a crowd of people in old-fashioned clothes, shaking their fists.

In the middle, a man was having a rope wound around his neck.

"Cool!" Zac said. "What's a gibbet, though?"

"I think it's the wooden frame that was used for hanging a person in the old days. Like when you play hangman," I said.

I hoisted the small coffin-box across to my other hip. It suddenly felt heavy and scratchy. I shivered again. Don't know why; I wasn't cold or anything.

We made our way back to the gate.

"Stupid name for a pub," said Zac, as we crossed back over the zebra crossing. He put on a grown-up voice: "Back soon, just popping out to The Noose and Gibbet for a beer …"

We burst out laughing again.

And all the way home, through the quiet streets, we thought up new names.

"The Goose and Giblet!"

"No … The Moose and Piglet!"

Chapter 2

We were soon back at my house. Mum was getting tea ready so we dashed upstairs to unpack our bag of things from the pub. Zac's always coming over to my house. He's my cousin and our families live very close to each other.

I blew the dust off a tankard. "This is perfect for the play. I bet no one's used it for years!"

Zac fished out an old cup. "Look, it's a picture of some posh king." He made a stupid face, squidging up his mouth.

"You look better like that!"

"Yeah, yeah, very funny …"

The lid of the coffin-box was nailed down. I prised it open with a screwdriver.

We peered inside.

"What is it?"

"Dunno." I shook something black out onto my bed. "Hey, it looks like a glove."

It was a glove, but not an ordinary one. It flopped over on my bed, and the fingers seemed to stretch out. I blinked – I must have just imagined that! The glove was made of old black leather, with crusty raised stitching. Metal studs ran along the outside edge.

"It smells odd," I said. "Kind of spicy."

I slid my hand inside the wide cuff and my fingers slipped halfway down inside. Then something odd happened; I felt as if my hand was being sucked in. "Eugh!" I said, trying to wriggle my hand out.

Zac sprang towards me. "Give us a go," he said and tugged the glove off my arm.

"That was weird," I began. "I hadn't even pushed my hand all the way in …"

Zac pulled the glove on, right up to his elbow. "Wow! Isn't it cool?" he said, running his fingers along the knobbles of dark metal on the outside edge.

Zac wandered around my bedroom, staring at his fingers like some girl checking her nail varnish. "I love it. It's just right for the play."

"The highwayman should wear it," I said. "That's Robert's part."

"Not necessarily," said Zac, roughly. "It should be me wearing it 'cos we found it."

He had an odd look on his face, like he was daring me to take the glove off him. "It's no good to you," he went on. "You're just the innkeeper. I'm a villager. A villager would wear it."

"Why?" I asked, putting the old box on my desk. I rather liked the box. I could fill it with my collection of joke things: itching powder, fart cushions and magic tricks; the sorts of things Zac and I always messed around with. "Mr Costello will decide anyway. I'll take all these props to tomorrow's rehearsal after school."

Zac was still admiring his black arm,

crunching and un-crunching the fingers. He strode around. "I need big black boots! A hat, I need a hat. And a horse! And if my horse is slow, I'll take a whip to her. Explode rockets under her. Push her till she falls and … and …" Zac's eyes looked odd, as if he couldn't focus properly.

"I feel like Cruella de ... what's her name in that film with the dogs?" He laughed softly. "Didn't *she* have long black gloves?"

"De Vil. Cruella de Vil," I said. "She wanted to kill the pups and make coats out of them. What's that got to do with anything?"

But Zac ignored me and went on gawping at his arm in the black glove.

"Zac?"

Zac turned and I saw his eyes gleaming with anger. "You just want to take it, don't you? Well, you won't. It's mine. Get it?" He rammed his gloved fist into the mirror on my desk. *Crunch!* The glass shattered.

"Zac!" Tears started in my eyes. "What's the matter with you, you idiot? Look what you've done!"

My lovely coloured mirror with sun rays was just a heap of blue and yellow glass shards. The whole frame was buckled and ruined.

My bedroom door flew open and Dillon, my little brother, appeared.

"Wassup?" he said.

"Go away, Dillon," I shouted.

He stared at me, then at Zac. "Mum said tea's ready," he faltered.

Then he was gone.

Zac glared at the door and then at me. I was waiting for him to say sorry, but he just flexed his gloved fingers.

A wave of hot anger burst out of me.

"That was a mean thing to do, Zac. Go home! And take off that stupid glove!"

Suddenly, Zac swung back his fist like a boxer.

I sprang out of the way as it swished past my face. I was horrified. This wasn't the Zac I knew. "What are you doing?" I shouted. "Get out!"

Zac stood very still, looking confused. Then he tugged off the glove and dropped it on my desk.

"Just forget it," he muttered.

Then he was gone.

Chapter 3

It felt odd walking to school on Monday without Zac. Normally he calls for me, but I set off early on my own. I was determined not to speak to him. Smashing my mirror like that – he had to say sorry before I could forgive him. I didn't see him for the whole day.

As I leaped onto the stage for the after-school rehearsal, I was certain that Zac would come and apologise, but he wasn't there. It was the usual chaos; Mr Costello, our drama teacher, was stressing about the set. Robert, the boy playing the highwayman, was struggling to pull on some big black wellies. Mrs Bentley was busy at the front. She was one of the mums who had offered to help with the costumes.

I said hi to some of the victims and villagers and pulled on my long boots and waistcoat. I lined up the old tankards on the bar.

Mr Costello sprang onto the stage. "Can I remind you all; we only have three weeks to cook this baby?"

Mr Costello sometimes said the weirdest things. He thought he sounded like a Hollywood director.

He saw my tankards from the pub. "Goodness, you've been busy, Shona. Where on earth did you find this lot?"

"In a pub that was closing down," I said.

Mr Costello nodded his approval, and then turned to the others.

"OK." He clapped his hands together. "Everyone here? Let's warm up. Close your eyes."

Mr Costello put on a spooky voice. "Now breathe deeply. Think yourselves into the play ... this is a local legend. We want the audience on the edge of their seats. Imagine the wind and rain on the common as our ruthless villain, the highwayman, comes galloping through the trees. Shona, you're listening for the highwayman's horse at the window. OK, Ella. Make me feel the darkness, the moon rising. Nice big voice, please."

Ella began to narrate the story:

"A cape of inky black he bore,
On a fine horse galloped he."

"OK, so the audience knows about the innkeeper waiting for the highwayman to arrive. Now – focus please, Shona."

On cue, I peeped out of an imaginary window and opened my mouth wide to show my excitement and fear. I love acting.

"'Tis bitter cold!" I called. *"I can feel villainy in my veins tonight!"*

"OK now," Mr Costello called. "Robert, swagger onto the stage. You are meeting Shona, the innkeeper."

Robert shuffled towards me with his bag of stolen goods over his shoulder.

"No, no, no!" shouted Mr Costello, clenching his fists and closing his eyes. "That's useless. You're supposed to be a wicked ruffian. You've got to LIVE the part!"

Robert tripped up in his wellies and clutched the edge of the tavern bar.

"I've a hideout on the common," he began in his wobbly voice. *"Where I hide me in the trees."*

Mr Costello jumped up and down. "Louder, Robert, louder! My cat could make a better job of this!"

I tried to keep a straight face but laughs began to explode all around me.

Robert's voice was a nervous squeak:

"For they'll never catch the Terror,
The Flintgate Man of Steel.
They'll never throw a noose around his neck ..."

Zac suddenly appeared next to me. He must have come in through the fire escape door. "Where's that glove?" he asked, roughly. "I need it."

Some of the cast were giggling again.

"Zac!" I said. "We're in the middle of rehearsing – "

"You've hidden it!" Zac hissed, shooting me a furious look and scrabbling around in the box behind the bar.

"Zac!" Mr Costello bellowed.

Zac thrust his hand inside the glove.

The laughs stopped.

Mr Costello strode over.

"Zac Edwards!" he snapped. "You're

always messing about and now you're late!" He pointed at the glove on Zac's arm. "What's that?"

Zac's eyes narrowed. "It's mine," he said, stroking the glove with his other hand, running his fingers over the studs like someone playing a piano. "It's part of my costume as a villager."

"Nonsense," said Mr Costello. "It's a gauntlet. Much better for the highwayman. Now, give it to Robert and we can get on with the rehearsal." He turned away.

"No!" Zac muttered.

"I beg your pardon?" Mr Costello turned back.

"I said, I won't!" Zac clenched his gloved fist.

He jumped down off the stage and walked out of the school hall.

"I, I, ..." Mr Costello's face was scarlet. "I will not be spoken to like that!"

"Any chance we could have a break, Mr C, while I measure up for costumes?" came the gentle voice of Mrs Bentley.

"Yes, yes," Mr Costello sighed. "Let's break. Ten minutes OK for you, Mrs B?" He frowned. "And Robert – you've got to really throw yourself into this part. I want to see a different person when you come back on stage. Got that?"

Chapter 4

Banging the hall doors behind me, I
ran down the empty corridor. OK, so I
was still cross with Zac, but if he didn't
apologise, Mr Costello would throw him
out of the play.

"Zac? Zac?"

There was no sign of him anywhere.

I dashed back into the hall past Mrs Bentley and a cluster of people wrapped in material. I leaped up the steps and rushed backstage. Where was Zac?

No one was in the wings. That only left the very back of the stage behind the black curtain. I pushed through. My eyes took a second to adjust to the semi-dark. There was someone there, right at the back. No, two people. One was Zac.

He was shoving someone up against the wall. I heard a gurgle and glimpsed an agonised face – a gasping mouth and popping eyes. Robert!

"What are you doing?" I shouted, rushing towards them. "Zac!"

I grabbed Zac's arm, my fingers closing round the hard leather glove. I tried to pull it away but it was useless; Zac's arm felt like solid wood.

Since when had Zac got so super-strong? Robert's face was purple.

"Zac! Stop it!" I landed a massive kick in Zac's shins.

Zac turned. His mouth was twisted into an evil half-smile and his eyes glared at me as if I were a complete stranger. Then he blinked and seemed to refocus, as if he'd suddenly realised who I was.

He let go and Robert flopped to the ground. "I had to sort it," he said, thrusting aside the curtain and disappearing back onto the stage.

I knelt down next to Robert. "What happened?" I asked.

"T... t ... tried to strangle me!" Robert croaked. He began coughing and rubbing the livid red marks on his neck. "Zac's an animal," he spluttered, staggering to his feet. "Attacked me for no reason. I'm going home!" He pushed open the fire exit door and was gone.

My head reeled. I got up slowly and caught sight of something on the wall.

I touched a dark powdery stain and an ice-cold chill spread through me. It was a shadowy imprint from Zac's glove.

A ghostly hand.

Chapter 5

I stepped through the curtain as the rehearsal was starting again.

I rushed to my place behind the bar as Ella droned on about the highwayman on his way to the inn. Mr Costello would be livid when he realised Robert had gone. Someone would have to read his lines.

But, on cue, a caped black figure sprang from the shadows. He was in full costume; hat, boots, wig, huge black sack over one shoulder and a mask over his eyes.

"A cape of inky black he bore ..." Ella began.

Mr Costello called out, "Right, right, that's lovely. Super. Good focus, Robert. Now you and the innkeeper make your plan."

The masked figure came striding towards me. This wasn't Robert. I'd seen that single black glove on one arm.

It was Zac.

"What are you doing?" I hissed.

But Zac shoved me aside and bellowed, *"I'll go out on the common and hide me in the trees."* His voice sounded deep. *"I'll raid the coach and grab the loot ..."*

He turned to the front of the stage and raised a fist in the air. I heard a little gasp from Mrs Bentley and the sound of pins scattering.

"I love it, I love it!" Mr Costello shouted. "Give me more of the pent-up panther!"

A ferocious shout from Zac rang out.
"They'll never catch the Terror,
The Flintgate Man of Steel.
They'll never throw a noose around his neck, and never make him squeal."

I know Zac's my cousin but he's never been great at acting. I couldn't believe it was him! He seemed so powerful and ... evil! A fierce scowl spread across his face; the Zac I knew never looked like that. Cold dread clutched at me.

"I'm a bruiser and a winner,
and I trap their living breath."

Zac yanked one of the inn customers towards him by the collar.

"Don't choke him, lad!" Mr Costello called good-naturedly as Dave's face turned scarlet. "You want his money. You'll do anything for money."

Zac spoke every line spot on. Mr Costello stood there with his mouth open, his face frozen with delight.

Clare, the maid from the inn, swept forward in her long red dress. *"Aye, I'll drink to thee!"* She fluttered her eyelashes at Zac. *"That's a fine jacket."* She leaned close.

Robert had always done this next bit like a timid wooden puppet. But not Zac! Zac pulled her roughly towards him with his hand around her waist.

"Let me alone, good Sir!" Clare struggled out of his grasp and whacked him away.

"Robert's really different!" she hissed as she rushed off the stage.

"Bring me a flagon of rum." Zac laughed a low rattling laugh. *"I feel good fortune is with me tonight!"*

When Zac eventually called for his horse, I thought I heard a horse whinny. A scent wafted from the stage; that spicy smell I'd noticed, from Zac's glove.

Zac grabbed a lantern off the props

table and ran past me, his top lip curled right back.

He laughed. *"The dark night beckons. There's rich pickings in the shadows for those who dare…"*

"That was stunning lad! Truly stunning," Mr Costello shouted.

And that's when Zac pulled off his mask.

Chapter 6

"Zac!" Mr Costello gasped. "But I don't understand. Where's Robert?"

"He was a whining waste of space!" Zac shouted, sprinting to the front of the stage. "I must fly!"

He opened his arms and launched himself off the stage into the pile of costumes at the front.

Zac had gone seriously mad.

Mrs Bentley screamed and cowered behind a rail of clothes.

"Get back here, Zac!" Mr Costello shouted.

Zac dashed over to some rucksacks on the hall chairs. He emptied them out onto the floor. "Ah, ha, the lightning tree!" he shouted. "A bag for you and a bag for me!"

He began shovelling mobile phones, books and pens into his black sack. He scooped up fistfuls of sandwiches out of a lunchbox and stuffed them into his mouth.

I rushed to the front of the stage and down the steps towards my snarling, strange cousin. "Zac, take the glove off. It's the glove, Zac."

He backed away. He kicked over chairs, scattering them in all directions. "Keep away from me, Badger Breath!"

I heard Mr Costello crying out, "Get help! Get the caretaker. Get anyone!"

"Take it off, Zac," I shouted.

"You'll never get the glove off me, never!" yelled Zac. "Never!"

I lunged forward to grab him, and that's when I noticed Mr Pemberton had walked in.

Chapter 7

"Zac Edwards!" Mr Pemberton, the head teacher, had a face of fury. "Put those things down!"

Zac threw the sack over his shoulder and squared up to Mr Pemberton. "Do not approach me, miserable man, for my power is vast!"

"How dare you!" The head teacher marched up to Zac.

Zac swiped at his face and grabbed his nose with the long glove.

"Arghhh!" Mr Pemberton's voice turned into a high squeal.

Two teachers and the caretaker appeared and rugby-tackled Zac.

"By dose is cubig off!" Mr Pemberton spluttered.

There was a massive PLOCK! as Zac's hand was pulled out of the glove and he was wrestled to the ground. The black glove hung from the head teacher's nose like a dangling black beak, and then dropped to the floor.

"Get this boy to my office this minute!" Mr Pemberton shouted, but in a rather shaky voice.

Zac was dragged out.

I was left there, looking down at the glove.

Chapter 8

Dad was making a bonfire in the garden when I got home. I slumped onto the garden bench. The glove was inside my rucksack, but it couldn't stay there. I knew I had to get rid of it – and quickly, before Zac came after it.

"What ya got?" Dillon asked, coming over, seeing me open my rucksack.

"Nothing to do with you, Dillon," I said, sharply.

But Dillon stood there, bobbing in front of me. "Is Zac coming round?"

"No, now GO AWAY!"

Dillon stomped back to Dad.

I walked to the end of the garden.

No one must ever wear this glove again, I thought, turning it over in my hands. I felt its thick, cool weight and gazed at the sheen on the black leather, gleaming in the evening light. Had it always been this shiny? Beautiful. The smell drifted up my nose. I watched my hands stroke the sides. Yes. Beautiful. Such a lovely smell. I held it right up to my face. I touched the cuff with my fingertips.

"Put this on. Go on," said a voice in my head.

My fingers slipped in. I watched my hand disappear inside. And something gently pulled my arm, tugging at the hairs.

"Be like me."

The voice!

"Be like me, wild and free ..."

There it was again.

I reeled back in horror. What was I doing?

I tugged at the glove but it was stuck firmly on my arm. I ran back to the house with the voice chanting inside my head, "I've come back ... I've come back ..."

I had to get this thing off!

I wedged the tips of the glove fingers in the back-door frame, closed the door a bit and pulled. Pain shot through my hand.

Keep pulling!

Dillon came running up. "What are you doing?" he said.

"Help me!" I shouted, still pulling. I couldn't budge that glove one inch. "It's like a wellie when it's stuck, Dillon."

Dillon laughed. He grabbed me round the waist. "Can I pull really hard?"

"Yes!" I shouted. "KEEP PULLING, DILLON!"

THWOCK!

Dillon and I flew into a flowerbed.

I staggered to my feet. The voice seemed to echo in my head. "Wear me ... Put me on ..."

I scooped up the glove, sprinted back up the garden to the bonfire and flung it into the heart of the flames.

HISSsssssssssssssssssssssssssssssss!

It sank into a pool of orange fire.

I stood there, panting and gaping at the purple arm-shape of flame as it twisted and coiled.

I'd done it!

A massive sound like a whip split the air, making us jump back and cling together.

Dad came rushing over. "Keep back!" he shouted. "Some of these branches are really dry."

I shivered and Dillon took my hand. "Didn't you like that glove?" he said.

"No," I said. "No, it was a bad thing, Dillon. Come on, let's help Dad."

And for the next hour we dragged armfuls of dead branches to Dad for him to feed to the hungry fire.

53

When Zac came round later, I let him in. I knew he must be in big trouble at school, but he looked so tired and pale that I didn't ask. He just said, in a flat voice, "Show me."

Of course, I knew exactly what he was talking about. It was getting dark but we walked up the garden and looked into the remains of Dad's smouldering fire.

"Is it in there?" asked Zac.

"Yes."

"I still feel like I want to wear it."

I sighed. "I know. Maybe that feeling will just, I dunno, wear off."

Zac stared into the ash. "I wonder whose glove it was," he said.

I frowned.

"I mean," Zac continued, "when I was wearing it, I felt like someone else …"

"Do you mean like a real highwayman, Zac?" I whispered.

"I don't know," Zac said. "Yes … maybe … I don't know."

"Well, it's gone now. Let's forget it, Zac."

It was easy to say, but I couldn't stop picturing the evil glove clenching and unclenching as I gazed into the smouldering fire.

Zac suddenly shivered, and I felt an icy chill shoot through me.

"Come on, let's go inside," I said. "Please Zac, pretend it never happened. It's over —"

We turned and walked back to the house. Was it really over? Were we really free of the terrible grip of the highwayman's gauntlet? Only time would tell ...